THE DOUBLEDAY *book of* PRINCESS STORIES

Geraldine McCaughrean
Illustrated by Lizzie Sanders

For Elinor and Emily
G.M.

For Princess Jo jo
L.S.

TRANSWORLD PUBLISHERS LTD
61-63 Uxbridge Road, London W5 5SA

TRANSWORLD PUBLISHERS (AUSTRALIA) PTY LTD
15-25 Helles Avenue, Moorebank, NSW 2170

TRANSWORLD PUBLISHERS (NZ) LTD
3 William Pickering Drive, Albany, Auckland

DOUBLEDAY CANADA LTD
105 Bond Street, Toronto, Ontario M5B lY3

Published l997 by Doubleday
a division of Transworld Publishers Ltd

Copyright © Geraldine McCaughrean 1997
Illustrations copyright © Lizzie Sanders 1997
Designed by Ian Butterworth

The right of Geraldine McCaughrean to be identified as the Author
of this work has been asserted in accordance with
the Copyright, Designs and Patents Act l988

A catalogue record for this book is available
from the British Library

ISBN 0 385 40783 1

Printed in Italy

THE DOUBLEDAY *book of*

PRINCESS STORIES

Geraldine McCaughrean
Illustrated by Lizzie Sanders

DOUBLEDAY
London · New York · Toronto · Sydney · Auckland

CONTENTS

THE GINGERBREAD BOY

Beneath blue skies, a King once planted a forest. In the centre of the forest lay a blue lake, and in the centre of the lake, a green island. In the centre of the island grew a rose garden encircled by a high wall, and in the wall was a silver gate locked with a golden key. In the garden stood a palace, and inside the palace lived a little girl called Princess Mine.

Her mother, the Queen, was dead. But once a week, on Sundays, her father, the King, rowed over to the island. For he owned the golden key. He and Mine would laugh and talk, picnic among the roses or play hide-and-seek on the stairs. It was not a prison, you see. Princess Mine had done nothing wrong. It was just that her father was so lonely, and loved her so much, he wanted to keep her all to himself, keep all her love for himself.

'You are Mine,' he said. 'And what is mine, I do not share.'

In fact he passed a law decreeing that anyone crossing the lake and entering in at the silver gate must DIE!

Every day Mine walked along the empty corridors, sat in the empty halls and looked at the empty garden. And though the rooms were full of toys, she was very, very lonely.

When she had played with all her toys, she went to the library and read stories. But the children in the stories all had pets, or brothers and sisters, or neighbours or uncles or aunts.

Friends.

The lonely Princess envied them dreadfully — even those with wicked stepmothers, or witches living next door.

One day, when Mine had read all the storybooks in the library, she browsed through other kinds — about history, gardening, science. . . In the middle of reading a cookery book, she got up and ran to the empty palace kitchen, flung open the larder door and took out flour, milk, sugar, ginger and a few other things besides. Then she mixed some gingerbread dough, and rolled it out on the golden kitchen table.

First she shaped a dog, with two raisin eyes. Then she made a cat with a liquorice tail. Next she made a chicken with parsley for feathers, and last of all — best of all — a boy with cherries for cheeks. Mine dusted her gingerbread friends with icing sugar, sprinkled them with tears of loneliness. . . then ran and fetched a book of magic from the library. Finally she found what she was looking for:

'With my hands I made you.
With my heart I want you.
With a wish may you come to LIFE!'

Mine read out the spell, first in a whisper, then in a shout.

Woof! Woof! The dog came to life.

Miaow! The cat came to life.

Pck-pck-pck! The chicken came to life — though it did have green feathers.

Last of all — best of all — the boy came to life and climbed down from the table. He was a little shorter than Mine, but he could run almost as fast, and whistle, which she could not.

'I shall call you Ginger,' said the Princess.

'I shall call you Mine,' said the boy.

Princess Mine and Ginger ate picnics in the rose garden, and ran races and threw sticks for the gingerbread dog. They played hide-and-seek with the gingerbread cat, and fed the gingerbread chicken on raisins and cherries. They sprawled in the library reading books and playing chess. They did some cooking, too.

But every Sunday, Ginger and the animals hid themselves up in the palace loft, so that the King, on his weekly visit, would not find out about them.

Then, one Tuesday morning, very early, the King set out across the lake towards the green island. Under his arm was a bright, ribbony parcel for Princess Mine. Today was her birthday, and he wanted to surprise her.

The boat bumped the bank. In the lock the golden key turned. Up the stairs climbed footsteps so quiet that no-one woke. The floorboards made no squeak, the hinges no creak, as the bedroom door swung open.

'WHAT'S THIS!?'

There on the bed, piled as high as six eiderdowns, were rabbits and chicks, kittens and puppies, kids, hamsters, doves and mice. And underneath them all were Mine and Ginger, sleeping hand-in-hand.

'PREPARE TO DIE!' bawled the King.

With a great fluttering, scurrying scamper, the animals dashed out past the King, leaving Mine and Ginger blinking in the morning light.

'WHAT HAVE YOU TO SAY FOR YOURSELF, DAUGHTER?' demanded the King.

Mine shrugged. 'That I was lonely before, and that now I am not. That this palace of yours was once a prison to me; now it's full of friends. Everyone needs friends, Papa. Even you.' And she got out of bed and kissed him.

Well, all of a sudden the King saw how wrong he had been to leave her all alone and lonely. But it was too late. There was nothing he could do.

'I passed a law and the law cannot be broken,' he said, tears rolling down his cheeks. 'Even I cannot break it. All these friends of yours must die, because they crossed the lake, and entered in at the silver gate.'

'No, they didn't!' said Mine with a laugh.

'It's no good, child. Lying won't save them. How else could they be here?'

'Come with me and I'll show you,' said Princess Mine. She led the King downstairs to the palace kitchen. And there she took flour and sugar, butter, ginger and milk, and made some dough. She rolled it out — bigger then ever before — and cut out the figure of a lady. Then she fetched the magic book from the library and read out the spell. There stood a Queen — a little

taller than the King, though not so fat. And she could whistle, which the King could not.

So Ginger and the animals did not have to die, because they had never crossed the lake, nor opened the silver gate.

But they did soon after. They all trooped outside, climbed into a rowing boat, and paddled across to the other bank. And there they joined the crowds flocking to see the wedding of the King to his gingerbread Queen.

You'll be glad to know that the two lived happily ever after. Because the King was not lonely any more.

Besides, the Queen could whistle, and she taught him how.

Golden Tree, Silver Tree and Copper

The western sea is silvery, but not so silvery as the fish who swim in it. Each year, trout swim up the long sea lochs past the high, grim walls of Scottish castles. And one such trout, once upon a time, swam always to the island of Eigg. There lived King Rowan and his wife, Silver Tree.

Once a year, the Queen asked a question of the sea trout, and her question was always the same:

> 'Fish who swims through all the sea
> Whose is the fairest face you see?'

The trout always answered as she expected:

> 'On all the shores of ocean blue,
> The fairest one by far is you',

which made the Queen happy, because she was vain.

16

Then King Rowan and Queen Silver Tree had a baby girl, and called her Golden Tree, that being the King's idea.

'Why? Is she more precious than me?' demanded the Queen.

'Not at all!' said the King. 'But see how golden her skin is compared with yours, pale as moonlight.' And he would not change his mind, no, he would not, which says something for the character of King Rowan, as his wife's temper was frightening.

Golden Tree had no such temper. She was as sweet and modest as the Queen was fierce and vain. To tell the truth, she was soon a lot more precious in the eyes of the King, the huntsmen, the gardeners and everyone on Eigg, who loved her dear as dear.

One year, when the trout were running, the tide brought in a Prince from the mainland in a boat with silver sails. 'I have heard tell of the beauty and sweetness of Princess Golden Tree,' he said to the King, 'and I have come to ask. . .' but then he saw Golden Tree and could not finish what he was going to say, because she was more beautiful than he had ever imagined.

'Daughter, daughter, do you like what you see of this Prince?' asked the King.

But Princess Golden Tree could not answer, because she had just seen Prince Pine, and she had never seen the like, neither awake nor in her dreams.

Meanwhile Queen Silver Tree was down at the lochside, calling out to the magic trout:

Fish who swims through all the sea,
Whose is the fairest face you see?'

And the sea trout replied:

'As Spring gives way to Summer
And age gives way to youth,
The Princess Golden Tree has now
The fairest face, in truth',

which did not please the Queen. She picked up a pebble and threw it at the trout. Then she went raging back to the castle and flung herself down on her bed. Her skin turned paler than ever, and she vowed she would die without the proper medicine.

'And what is that, my dear?' said the King in great alarm.

'The heart of Golden Tree, roasted on a silver platter!'

Aghast, King Rowan thought quickly. 'Golden Tree is gone, my dear. A Prince came to ask for her, and I let her go — to the mainland where beauty is hardly noticed, as you know.'

'Fetch her back and kill her!' groaned Silver Tree. 'For her heart is all that can save me!'

So the King hurried down to the harbour, where Prince and Princess were still talking and not talking, gazing into each other's eyes. The King drew his dagger. . .

'Quick! Quick!' he said, cutting through the ship's mooring rope. 'Sail for the mainland! Your mother is so sick with jealousy of your beauty, Golden Tree, that I'm afeared you may die of it!'

Then, as the two sailed away, King Rowan went to the butcher's shop and bought a deer's heart and took it home for tea, saying it was the heart of Golden Tree.

A year later, when the trout were running, Queen Silver Tree went down to the sea loch again.

'Fish who swims through all the sea,
    Whose is the fairest face you see?'
And the trout replied:
    'In all my runs along the shores,
    I never see the like of yours
    Until I reach where Golden Tree
    Sits with her baby on her knee.'

The Queen hurled a stone at the trout and stormed back to the castle. This time she did not take to her bed, but boarded a ship and, taking the helm, steered it across the ocean swell. Wind and rain in her face, she pointed ahead through mist and spray, shouting commands at the crew. No Viking raider ever ploughed more menacingly over the ocean swell. Above the castle of Princess Golden Tree, the gulls shrieked out a warning.

Prince Pine was away reaping heather, but Golden Tree saw the longship and knew the figure at the helm. So she locked every castle door and put her baby, little Copper Tree, safe in the cradle.

'Golden Tree, my dear!' called her mother at the door. 'You left so suddenly, I had no time to wish you well. Now I hear you have a baby! Let me in to see this granddaughter of mine!'

But Golden Tree pretended she could not open the door. 'Wait a little till my husband comes home!' she called through the lock. 'He has the keys to the door.'

'I will! But while we wait, won't you just put your little finger through the keyhole, so that I may kiss it?'

Golden Tree could see no harm in that, so she put her little finger through the keyhole and — ouch! — felt the stab of a rose thorn. The thorn was poisoned, and down she fell, as cold as death. And all that greeted Prince Pine on his return was the crying of his child and the sight of his wife on the floor.

He thought there was no living without her, and he found there was no parting from her loveliness. So, telling no-one, he made a coffin of glass for her and placed her in it, within a locked room, and kept the only key himself. In his sorrow, little Copper Tree was his only comfort, but though he loved her dearly as she grew, even she could not make him smile, not any more.

One day, when Prince Pine set off a-planting trees, Copper Tree found his keys and ran after him. But he was gone. Being an inquisitive little girl, she went about the castle matching each key to each lock, until she came to the door-that-must-stay-locked. Boldly she went inside.

And there, to her great amazement, she saw a lady encased in a coffin of glass and set about with fresh flowers (which the Prince brought every day from the hillside). It did not take her long to guess: this must be her mother!

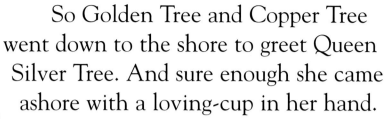

So Golden Tree and Copper Tree went down to the shore to greet Queen Silver Tree. And sure enough she came ashore with a loving-cup in her hand.

'Drink to our meeting, daughter dear! Drink to our friendship, granddaughter dear!' and she held out the goblet — full to the brim with poison.

'We have a custom in these parts,' said Copper Tree, in her small, tinkling voice. 'A visitor must always drink first. So drink yourself, Grandmamma, and then we shall drink after.'

'Yes,' said Golden Tree. 'Drink.'

'Yes,' cried the gulls flying overhead. 'Drink.'

'Drink,' said the captain of the ship she had steered.

'Drink,' said the crew.

'Drink,' said the very stones of the beach.

'Drink,' said Prince Pine galloping down to the shore.

'Yes,' said King Rowan stepping down from the ship in person. 'Drink.'

So Queen Silver Tree drank, and fell dead just where she had meant her daughter and granddaughter to lie. They put her aboard the longship and set it out to sea, and the tides took it who-knows-where, out on the treeless ocean.

So Prince Pine and Golden Tree lived happily for ever, and Rowan was a true friend to them. But their best friend of all was Copper Tree, who learned from the sea trout to be wise. In fact, she learnt such wisdom that when the sea trout told her that she was the fairest in the world, she said, 'Get away with your flattering, you foolish fishy, or I'll cook you for supper!'

SPOILED

There was once a Princess whose parents loved her too much. They tried to make her happy every minute of every day, and so they brought her everything she asked for, and never told her, 'No'. There was a saying among the palace servants: 'What Winnie wants, Winnie must have.' And there seemed no end to what Winnie wanted.

On the day before her seventh birthday, her mother, the Queen, looked around the bedroom covered with toys and sighed. 'Whatever can we give you, darling Winnie? You seem to have everything already.'

Winnie took a deep breath: 'I want a gold-and-silver dress

and lots of pretty jewels and I want long golden ringlets. I want it always to be my birthday and I want to know everything, without ever going to school!'

Her father, the King, sighed. For the very first time, he shook his head and said, 'No. I'm sorry, Winnie. There's no money left in the exchequer, and your hair is the hair you were born with. And as for school. . .'

But Winnie was not listening. At the sound of that terrible word — NO — she had slammed out of the room, out of the palace and away into the wide world. 'If they won't give me what I want, I shall just have to get it for myself!'

She walked and walked until she came to a town and, in the centre of the town, a tall house. Parked outside was a glass coach with six white horses, and beside the coach stood an elderly lady.

Down the steps came the prettiest girl that Winnie had ever seen, wearing . . . a beautiful dress of gold and silver lace!

At once Winnie said, 'Oh! How I WANT that dress!'

The old lady looked from Winnie to the pretty girl and back again, then she sadly sighed and said, 'Go indoors, Cinderella. What Winnie wants, Winnie must have.'

So the girl cast her sad blue eyes in the direction of the skyline, where a distant castle twinkled with lights. 'Now I shall never go to the ball!' she sighed before turning back inside and taking off the dress. Winnie put it on. It fitted perfectly. And the skirts of gold and silver lace swished so sweetly as Winnie walked, that she could not hear Cinderella quietly sobbing on the step of the glass coach.

Outside the city, her path lay through a forest. All night Winnie walked until, at dawn, a tangle of rose briars blocked her way. Someone was hacking through them, for the briars shook to the sound. 'Are you going to take long?' called Winnie. 'I am in a fearful hurry.'

The most handsome Prince she had ever seen emerged and leaned forward on his sword to catch his breath. The sword hilt shone with every kind of precious gem. 'Good morning, maiden. It may take me many days to cut through these briars. You had better go another way.' Winnie did not hear him. She was too much intent on gazing at his sword.

'Oh, let me see! All those pretty jewels! How I do WANT them!'

The prince turned a little pale, and his smile faded. 'But the enchantment! The Sleeping—' Then, sighing, he bowed low and presented her with his sword. 'What Winnie wants, Winnie must have.' With only one more longing look at the turrets of a palace almost hidden behind the entanglement of briars, the prince mounted his horse and galloped away.

With the jewelled sword through her sash, Winnie danced off across the desert to where the sea pounded on a rocky shore. There, in the window of a high tower, sat Rapunzel, the happiest woman Winnie had ever seen. Her golden hair trickled down the wall, intertwining with passion flowers, and she whispered to Winnie, 'I hope one day you are as happy as I am, little girl.'

'I would be if I had hair like yours,' said Winnie, her voice sour with jealousy.

Rapunzel's smile melted away. 'But what when he comes?' she started to say. 'What when he cannot find the Golden Stair to climb?' Then Rapunzel sighed the saddest of sighs. 'What Winnie wants, Winnie must have.' And she dropped down from her window a pair of golden scissors. 'Take whatever you want.'

So Winnie climbed and snipped, climbed and snipped every last ringlet of hair. She fastened it to her own with tendrils of passion flowers and went on her way.

At the bottom of the world she came to a dreadful place where the Cog Wheel stands which turns the Earth. And there, straining with all his might to hold the wheel still, stood The Man Who Knows.

'Oo. It's so cold here,' said Winnie.

'Winnie wants it always to be her birthday,' said The Man Who Knows. 'So this side of the world must always be winter, so that her side may have the tenth of June for ever.'

Winnie was not listening. 'I came here because I want to know everything, without having to go to school.'

'Mmmm. Well, I will tell you just four things,' he said. 'Far away, in a big town, Cinderella is crying. Winnie wanted her dress. So now Cinderella cannot go to the ball.

Deep in the forest, Sleeping Beauty lies spellbound for ever. The prince who should have woken her has no sword to cut through the briars.

High in a tower, Rapunzel sits crying. Her prince came back for her, but had no golden plait to climb and so he rode away.'

'Stop! Stop!' cried Winnie. 'Is everyone in the world unhappy because of me?' She covered her eyes.

'No, no, my dear! Your mother and father are quite relieved you went away. Even now they are saying, "What a mercy, not to have to keep buying Winnie what she wants." '

'I didn't want to know that! I don't want it to be true! I don't want any of it to have happened!'

'Ah!' said The Man Who Knows. 'To make that so, I'd have to turn the world back to yesterday. I've never done that before.'

'Oh, turn it!' begged Winnie. 'Let me help! Oh, I do so WANT to undo today!'

'What Winnie wants, Winnie must have,' laughed the man. And, with a gigantic push, they rolled the world back one whole day.

It spun so fast that Winnie fell dizzily to the ground. When she opened her eyes, she was lying in her own bed. 'Mother, Mother! What day is it? I must know what day it is!'

'Why, it's the ninth of June, of course,' said her mother. 'The day before your birthday.'

'Oh, thank goodness!' said Winnie. 'I do so want. . .'

Her mother sighed. 'Yes, Winnie? And what do you want now?'

'To have a party!' cried Winnie. 'A party for you and for the servants and for everyone at school! To say thank you for all the lovely things I've got! That's all. Oh, let me, please!'

Her mother sighed, but it was a sigh of deep contentment. 'Then what Winnie wants, Winnie shall have.'

PRINCESS HIGH-AND-MIGHTY

'All men are fools,' said Princess High-and-Mighty. 'The only man I would ever marry is the man I couldn't see or hear!' And so saying, she took herself off to a high tower with twelve windows, saying she would not — no, she would never — marry.

The King, her father, was appalled. His only child not marry? There would be no grandchildren to inherit the throne! Worse still, he would have to put up with her bad temper for the rest of his days. High-and-Mighty scared her father, not least by her habit of screwing up one eye and glaring at him with the other. When she did that, he knew she could see every grey hair of his beard, every breadcrumb left over from breakfast, every frayed thread in his coat. She had the eyesight of a hawk, and much the same nature.

The King racked his brains. 'So. You want a man you can neither see nor hear, do you?' he thought. 'Very well, young lady. I shall take you at your word.' And he issued a proclamation:

My daughter will marry the man who can
reach her unseen and unheard.

Sucking his pen he added, as a footnote:
(Three tries permitted.)

To his surprise, men began to arrive by the dozen. Some were local, some came from abroad. They came because she was a Princess, of course, and very rich. They came because, if they married her, they would one day wear the crown of Polgarslovia. It would have been nice if they had wanted High-and-Mighty for herself, thought the King . . . but then who would?

They crept up to the tall tower on hands and knees. But before they were within one mile of it, a herald would come galloping with a letter from Princess High-and-Mighty. The letter simply said, *Seen you.*

They approached by night, falling into bogs, twisting their ankles in rabbit holes. But before they were within a mile of the tower, a beam of light would shine on them from one of the twelve windows and a voice would shout, *Heard you!*

They approached in hot-air balloons, but no sooner were they within range, than Princess High-and-Mighty fired an arrow from one of the twelve windows, and the balloons sank slowly to earth. They came in camouflage green, and disguised as sheep and cows. They came in covered wagons, and slung underneath their horses. But the Princess spotted each and every one, and her contempt for men grew, along with her determination never to marry.

Frank was a forester. He knew nothing about Princesses, and cared even less. All he cared about was animals. So when one day he saw a crow being mobbed by starlings, he swung his jacket to scare them away, then carried the bird about on his

shoulder until it was well again. Another time he found a vixen in a trap, and let her go. She followed him about after that, like a dog. Then once there was a fire in the forest, and he saw a toad cut off by a ring of flame, and actually braved the heat and smoke to rescue it.

'I think,' said the toad (much to Frank's surprise), 'that one good turn deserves another.'

'I agree,' said the crow on Frank's shoulder.

'We should help him find his fortune,' said the vixen.

'I never knew you could talk!' said Frank.

'You never asked,' said the vixen. 'In fact, that's your trouble. You never ask anything of life, and yet you deserve wealth and happiness more than any human I know. You should try for the hand of Princess High-and-Mighty. We would help you.'

Frank shook his head. 'No, thank you. The only girl I ever saw to my liking lives over yonder in a high tower with twelve windows. Don't know who she is, but I know she doesn't like men going close. She's beautiful. Nose like a tortoise, hair like a squirrel — and a way of looking at you like a hawk in the sky!'

'Her, then,' said the animals and looked at each other, rolling their eyes.

The crow was magic, of course. She built a nest in a tree, then told Frank to cut down the tree and chop it into firewood. This he loaded aboard a horse and cart. Then the crow put Frank inside one of her eggs in the nest, the vixen barked, and the horse trotted off towards the high tower.

When it was still a mile away, Princess High-and-Mighty heard the cart coming, and looked out of one of the twelve windows. She saw the cart, the firewood, the nest and, in the nest, the eggs. 'I see you, fool-in-the-egg!' she shouted.

'Ah! What a voice! Like a bittern booming!' sighed Frank. 'I must try again!'

The toad was magic, of course. She opened her mouth as wide as an umbrella, and swallowed Frank down. Then she hopped into a river, swam down to the bottom, and crept slowly, slowly along it towards the tall tower.

Though it happened a mile away, Princess High-and-Mighty heard a splash and looked out of one of the twelve windows. She saw the river, saw the ripples, saw the toad on the river bed. 'I see you, fool-in-the-toad!' she shouted.

'Ah! The eyesight of a fly!' sighed Frank. 'I must reach her!'

The vixen was magic, too, of course. 'Stand still,' she said, 'and trust your friends.' She flicked Frank with her ginger brush, and turned him, then and there, into a book with a thousand pages. Carrying the book in her soft mouth, she set it down in front of the tall tower before trotting away.

Princess High-and-Mighty looked out of the twelve windows and saw the book. Her sharp eyes counted the thousand pages and read the title: *A Book of Princesses*.

Down her spiral stairs she ran and out to where the book lay. Scooping it up eagerly, she found herself holding . . . a young man in her arms.

'You're even cleverer than I am,' she said.

'Not clever enough to know your name,' said Frank. 'What is it?'

'Rose, though they all call me High-and-Mighty.'

'Why?' asked Frank. 'Rose is a beautiful name — almost as beautiful as you.'

The King came speeding from the palace in an open coach, shaking the reins himself, urging on the horses. In the coach rode a fox, a crow and a toad. 'What's this I hear? Someone passed the test? Someone did it? Will you marry him?'

'Yes, Father, I rather think I will,' said Princess Rose, then added nervously, 'if he wants me to.'

'I rather think I do,' said Frank, and the vixen and the crow and the toad barked and cawed and hopped about with delight, till the King's coach rocked on its wheels.

Their happiness was nothing compared with the joy of Frank and Rose after they were married. Bride and groom lived together in the tall, tall tower. When they sat hand-in-hand on its window sill and looked at the view, they could both see all the way to Ever After. And Rose and Frank liked what they saw.

MERMAID PRINCESS

He thought it was a fish at first — something big and strange washed ashore out of the deep ocean. But when he got closer, he saw it was too silvery to be a dead thing. And there were several of them — a whole shoal of scaly sheaths with huge fluke fins, strewn here and there on the beach. Ivan was a fisherman, but he had never seen fish like these in all his days at sea.

Bending to pick one up, he was suddenly bowled off his feet by a pack of young girls, stark naked but for the shell wreaths in their hair, who leapt from behind rocks and ran for the sea. Mermaids, come ashore to play in the rock pools, had taken off their tails to move more easily on dry land. Now they snatched up their tails and fled, barging him to the ground, plunging into the surf with cries like seal cubs.

But Ivan held tight to the tail in his hands, and clutched it to his chest as the sand and spray flew. When he opened his eyes again, a young girl stood in front of him, hands outstretched, pleading for her tail. 'I shall die if I don't have it,' she said.

'Never. You come home with me. I think I might spare you a plate of sardines. Fancy! A real mermaid! I'll make a fortune!'

The mermaid's seal-brown eyes brimmed with tears. 'I shall die if I don't go back on the falling tide,' she said. 'Will you make such a fortune from a dead mermaid?'

Ivan saw how she was trembling, how her tears spilled, how her hands dropped back to her sides in helpless despair.

'I'm sorry,' he said, laying the tail down at her feet. 'I'm a poor man. Sometimes I lose sight of other people's needs in thinking of my own. Go. Before you miss the tide.'

Delightedly the mermaid slithered into her tail and flung herself headlong into the surf. She was beyond the seventh wave before she raised her head above the water again and called, 'Come with me! My father will want to thank you. You won't be sorry you let me go, I promise!'

Ivan did not know what came over him. He was not a good swimmer and he was still dressed in his fisherman's sweater and seaboots. But he found himself wading out to sea, just to touch the fingertips she stretched out to him. And once he had touched those fingers—

SPLOOSH!

It did not matter that a wave broke over his head and swirled him off his feet. All the while she kept hold of his hand, he was able to breathe — even under the water!

'What's your name?' he shouted, and saw his words, bubble-shaped, rush towards the turquoise surface.

'Marina. Princess Marina.'

It was true. He had not just found a mermaid on the beach; he had found the mermaid among mermaids — only daughter of the King of the Ocean! On the slopes of an undersea mountain range whose peaks broke surface to form a chain of islands, Ivan was introduced to King Neptune.

'He let me go, Father! He could have showed me off like an oddity at the zoo, but he let me go. Wasn't that wonderful of him?'

The King, whose couch was the hull of a sunken galleon and whose belt was made of lobster pots and buoys, pointed his trident at Ivan. 'You are as welcome here as is the sight of our daughter safe and well. Accept our meagre hospitality and stay as long as you wish!' At that, a mermaid blew a conch shell, and the eerie noise of it set the ocean trembling, fetching from every crevice and spinney of weed a host of strange creatures who came to fetch Ivan his every wish.

He ate fruit from the golden weed trees, honey from the floors of the undersea, and shark meat brought home by the great mer-hunters, daring as toreadors. A million brilliantly coloured fish danced in mesmerizing clouds around his head, while cleaner-fish sipped every last grain of dust from his hair and clothes. All the while, Princess Marina kept tight hold of his hand, and told him stories of drowned cities, and great sea storms, of ghost ships, and of meteorites splashing into the sea.

'Stay, won't you?' she said, unsettling him once again with those doleful eyes. 'I don't care a fig for our pale-skinned, hairless, sleek men of Mer. I've always dreamed of a husband from the place of sunshine, with a rough red beard like yours and strong muscles made by good hard work. Stay with me — or do you have a wife waiting for you on the land?'

'I don't,' said Ivan. 'Nor did I ever see a maiden as beautiful as you. But I am from that world and you are from this. You would only have to let go of my hand . . .'

'I never would! Not once! Not even when I fell asleep!'

'. . . And I would drown like a fish on a slab. How could I work with only one hand, no nets and no-one to buy my fish? No. Take me back where I belong. I shall never forget you or your kingdom, but where could we make our home, us two?'

Underwater it is impossible to see a mermaid's tears, but Ivan could taste Marina's — saltier than the surrounding sea. He bowed to the King of Oceans, thanked him for his royal welcome, and led Marina unwillingly away towards shallow water and dry land. The tide was just turning as they kissed goodbye.

'Let me stay with you!' pleaded Marina. 'Perhaps I could live for a year or two on land, if you sprinkled me with water . . .'

'People would stare. People would pry,' said Ivan. 'People would never leave us alone. Go quickly, and let's pretend we dreamed each other.'

For a great many days, back at the slopes of Neptune, Marina did not speak. Her father grew anxious about her. He knew she was thinking of the dry-land fisherman. 'Say the word, daughter, and I will wreck his fishing boat far from shore and fetch him back here to you.'

Marina shook her head. 'No. But if I cannot look after him as a dry-land wife, perhaps I could still take care of him in other ways.'

That is why, when Ivan next wound in his nets he found, in the mouths of the fishes, precious gleaming gems, ancient coins, pearls from the oyster beds.

Far from being poor, Ivan became rich, and the young local girls made themselves look pretty and walked pointedly up and down the wharf when he was unloading, hoping to catch his eye. But Ivan never gave them a second look. It seemed he would never marry at all. In fact he grew thin and dishevelled for a time, as if he had too much on his mind to take proper care of himself.

Sometimes he tangled daisies in the mesh of the nets before he let them down. He was doing this when he accidentally knocked his old torn smock over the side into the sea. It was returned to him, on the next trip, clean and mended, like new. And on Fridays, the catch he brought up had been cooked on the volcanoes on Undersea, herb-sprinkled, crispy and delicious. After that, he lowered down books and mirrors and pretty tin cups — the sort of thing, he thought, that mermaids might find it hard to come by.

The other fishermen did not know what to make of him. 'He talks to himself,' they said. 'He throws things over the side. He talks to himself all the while — or that seal that's always swimming round his boat.'

They could see he was no longer happy on shore. The old fishwives told him, 'You work too hard, Ivan! Why take your boat out every day? In all weathers! It's not as if you have a wife or children to support. Don't work so hard!'

But Ivan would simply look at them with eyes as round and moist as a seal's, and murmur, 'Children, yes, children. That would have been nice . . . I must be going now. I must get out on the water.'

'Sea fever, that's his trouble,' said the fishermen, scowling. 'Sometimes the sea gets into a man's blood . . .'

Ten years later, one stormy day, when all the fishing boats ran for harbour, Ivan's did not arrive home.

The fishermen took off their caps in sorrow. The fishwives crumpled their aprons and said, 'We knew it, we knew it all along.' And several of the young girls shed a secret tear to think of young Ivan, gone.

But then they heard it — everyone heard it, no mistaking — the muffled clamour of bells ringing under fifty fathoms of sea.

'That's a sea wedding,' mused the oldest fishwife. 'Them's wedding bells. That's one of the mermaids marrying, for sure.' Then she suddenly smiled, and her smile passed along from face to face. The fishermen threw their caps in the air, the fishwives waved their aprons, and everyone shouted together out towards the sea: 'Congratulations, Ivan! Good luck to you!'

SUMIO WHO FELL FROM THE MOON

One night when the moon was full, a little old man and a little old lady held hands and wished a wish. They wished for a child, because all life long they had only had each other.

Suddenly there was a crash behind them, among the bushes. At first they thought some wild animal was prowling through the bamboo. But when they heard the crying, and went to look, they found a little baby girl. The old lady picked her up and gave her a kiss — also, a name as sweet as any kiss: Sumio. Then they took her indoors and loved her as if she were their own daughter. Sumio loved them just as much.

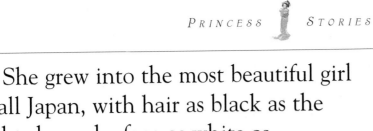

She grew into the most beautiful girl in all Japan, with hair as black as the night sky and a face as white as moonlight. The news of her loveliness spread, like water spilled from a jar, and poets came from far and wide to gaze at this house, hoping for a glimpse of Sumio.

Far away, the Emperor heard tell of Sumio's beauty. 'I may have her for my wife,' he yawned, scratching his grey beard. 'Tell her to come, so that I can take a look at her.'

But Sumio did not come, would not come, and the Emperor waited in vain.

'Well, no-one else shall have her,' complained the Emperor, picking his yellow teeth. 'If I must, I shall go and fetch her myself.'

He called at Sumio's house, and was given green mint tea and macaroons. 'I mean to do you the honour of marrying you,' he told Sumio (who was even lovelier then he had imagined).

'No, thank you, sir,' replied Sumio politely. 'That is not possible.'

The Emperor sucked tea out of his moustache and scowled. 'I don't think you quite understand me,' he said. 'I say I shall marry you and so we shall be married.'

Sumio bowed politely. 'I regret we cannot. You see, your Imperial Highness, I am the Princess of the Moon. My nurse rocked the cradle too hard and I fell down here from my country in the sky. But very soon my people will be coming to take me back to the Land of Silver Soil.' And she opened the door to let him out.

The Emperor scuffed his heels all the way down the hill. When he reached the bottom, he turned and pointed his imperial finger at Sumio.

'Have I not captured castles?' he shouted. 'Have I not captured cities? Prepare to marry, Sumio! I shall return with my army tonight! Princess of the Moon, indeed! Pish!'

The little old lady and the little old man might have begged Sumio to agree. Their daughter married to the Emperor? Think of the honour and riches it would bring them!

But the little old woman closed the windows and the little old man barred the door. 'If you don't want to go with him, you shan't,' he said and his wife agreed.

At sunset the Emperor arrived with seven battalions of troops, and circled the hill as if it were the mightiest of castles. He brought a large box to put the Princess in, and barrels of gunpowder to destroy the little house on the hill.

At midnight, he started up the path. The bamboo trembled at the stamp of soldiers' feet. The stars blinked with astonishment at the sight of so many troops. The moon was just

rising, and its light glinted on a thousand
sharp swords, a thousand pointed spears, ten
thousand iron-tipped arrows.

Sumio opened the door and stepped outside. The little old
man held her hand on one side, the little old lady held her hand
on the other. She looked even more lovely in the milky
moonlight, and fireflies swooped around her head.

'Give yourself up to me, Sumio!' called the Emperor. 'For I
never want a thing but I get it!'

All of a sudden, a broad moonbeam fell across the hill. Like a
river of milk it shone, the Princess on one side, the Emperor and
his guards on the other. The soldiers moved forward to seize her
— and stopped short. They tugged and wriggled. But their boots
seemed to be stuck to the ground. They could not take another
step.

'Grab her, you fools! What are you waiting for?' boomed the Emperor, and strode forward himself. But — 'Oh! Help!' — he sank up to his ankles in moonlight, up to his knees, up to his waist, up to his chest. He struggled and wriggled, but the sticky moonlight only sucked at his silken sleeves and grey hair.

As seven battalions stared in amazement, a second moonbeam unfurled, like a bolt of white silk unrolling. It had no sooner touched the ground than it stiffened into a silver chute, and down from the moon slid a cascade of warriors in silver armour with stars on their breastplates and moondust in their long hair. Down the slope galloped a pearly chariot drawn by the dappled moon-horses who stopped in front of Sumio; the charioteer lifted her aboard.

'We must take my friends here, too,' she sighed, helping the little old couple into the chariot, 'because I love them as dearly as my own mother and father.'

The Emperor puffed and panted. The Emperor fretted and fumed, wriggled and writhed. His soldiers pulled and his Chancellor pushed. But he stayed stuck fast in the river of gluey moonlight as his would-be bride sped away into the night sky.

And he could not get free till morning.

TOWN PALACE, COUNTRY PALACE

There was once a King who had so many children that his palace was full to bursting. There were Princesses in the kitchen and Princes in the parlour, more in the morning room and lots in the lofts. So the King took out his chest of gold and said, 'Let all but the littlest leave home. Then your mother and I can have some peace!'

Some took trains to distant countries. Some bought boats and lived on them. Some rented palazzos by the canals of Venice. Some looked in the newspapers and found castles for sale.

But Princess Adelaide and Princess Ottaline chose to build their own palaces from top to bottom, and one chose the country and one chose the town.

'Mine will be finer then fine,' said Ottaline. 'Mine will be grander than grand!' And she built in concrete, glass and steel at the top of the highest hill in the city. 'I want soaring pillars, and ceilings as high as the sky. Every room must be bigger than my father's whole palace, every cupboard as big as a room. I want lift-shafts and spires, I want cloisters and choirs. I want it all finished by June!'

She employed every builder, painter and plasterer in the land. By every strike of the hour on her huge gilded clocks, tradesmen and delivery boys arrived with braids and brocades, satins and rattans, panelling and chandeliers. Ottaline stood at the top of the stairs and shouted, 'Put it there! No, there! Now try there!'

She hired everybody in town as palace servants, because there was so much housework to do. But on the day all the work was finished, she had the biggest palace in the land. That same night, she sent everybody away.

'Can't live here,' she said. 'You aren't royal like me. You must live in the town and only come up here to work each day.'

The servants mumbled and grumbled because the hill was very steep and they would have to get up very early. 'How much will you pay us?' they asked.

'Pay you? I've no money left to pay you! Don't you realize how much this castle cost to build? Besides, I'm a Princess, and everybody wants to work for a Princess in a palace like mine.'

Away went the servants, shaking their heads and rubbing their hands (because the weather was getting cold).

Out in the country, Princess Adelaide found a pretty spot for her palace — but then she had no idea where to begin. So she asked the insects and the animals for their help. 'How should I build?' she asked.

'With paper,' said the wasp and showed her how to chew woodchips and make grey paper and mould a city of tiny rooms each big enough for a wasp.

'That's not how,' said the badger, and he showed her how to dig a sett and line it with fresh grass every day and make it cosy for cubs.

'That's not how,' said the rooks, and they showed her how to weave a nest out of twigs and balance it high up in a tree.

'That's not how,' said the water vole, and he showed her how to burrow in the riverbank — though the squirrels were of the opinion she should live in a hollow tree.

Adelaide did her best to please them all, and soon she had built a sett halfway up a hollow tree, overhanging a river and divided into paper chambers. It was very cosy and she was never short of company, for her animal friends came day and night and danced to the fiddling of the grasshoppers.

Then winter arrived.

Up on the hill, it shook at Ottaline's windows. Draughts howled around the enormous rooms, and set the curtains streaming like sails and the doors banging. Thunder boomed like cannonfire over the roofs. She huddled in bed with her crown on her head, and tried to feel regal. But nobody came when she called, for it was no weather to climb the hill, especially for no wages.

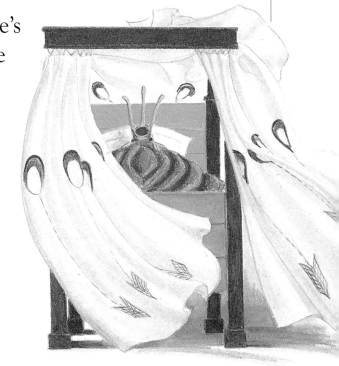

The fires blew out in the grates. The candles blew out in their sconces. And then Ottaline would have gladly crept into a cupboard with her eiderdown, except that the cupboards were all as big as rooms and full of shadows, and she was too afraid to unlatch them and let out the dark. No water came to the taps, because the palace was so high up. And the cows she kept for her cream and the horses she kept for her carriage roamed off in the darkness to keep the wind out of their ears.

Nobody ventured out those cold, dark days. What, climb that hill to be shouted at? So they stayed in their small, warm cottages and said, 'What a waste of gold to give it to one like that.'

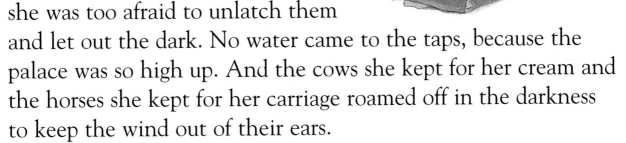

Meanwhile, out in the country, down by the stream, Princess Adelaide was snug and warm in her honeycomb palace, curled up among all her friends while the storm raged outside. Only the wasps were missing.

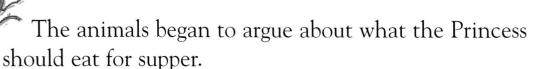

The animals began to argue about what the Princess should eat for supper.

And whom she should marry.

And when she should go to sleep.

'Excuse me,' said Adelaide, 'but I don't want to go to sleep.'

'Oh, but you must, you must,' said the hedgehog. 'All winter. Eat now. Eat. Eat! Then go to sleep for a good four months.'

'The question is, has she stored enough nuts?' said the squirrels.

'Excuse me, but I don't like nuts,' said Adelaide.

'Worms and beetles,' said the badger. 'Worms and beetles, then she'll be fat enough in the spring to marry my nephew.'

'Of course, she may die in winter, like the wasps . . .'

'Excuse me!'

At this point, the palace, which was built halfway up a hollow tree, out of twigs and paper and feathers and turf, fell down, tree and all, into the stream below, washing along like a raft.

They sailed all night, till the tree ran ashore on the city quayside, at the bottom of a hill. Seeing a blaze of light high up, the animals naturally ran away, while Adelaide climbed towards it.

Halfway up the hill, she met Ottaline coming down, and hand-in-hand they walked to the railway station through the driving rain. They caught the train home, where the King and Queen gave them crumpets and kippers for tea. Oddly enough, all the other Princes and Princesses seemed to be visiting that night.

'We have been thinking of building an East Wing,' said the King. 'For the Princesses.'

'And a West Wing,' said the Queen. 'For the Princes.'

'Plenty of room for everyone,' they said, and nothing more was ever mentioned of anyone leaving home.

EAST OF THE SUN, WEST OF THE MOON

There was once a man so poor that he had nothing to feed his children, and barely the firewood to keep them warm. One night, when snow lay level with the windows, and the wind howled in the chimney, someone came beating at the door.

There, towering over the man as he opened the door, was a huge polar bear. 'I am Prince of Bears. Give me your youngest, sweetest girl, and I shall give you home and heat and food to feed your family, and riches besides.'

'No! No!' said the man. 'Take Molly? We'd sooner starve!'

But Molly ran up, her cloak already round her shoulders. 'If it is for the good of you, then how can it be bad for me?' Then, kissing her father goodbye, she took the Bear's paw and went out into the blizzard.

She thought at first that the Bear meant to eat her, but he simply took her on his back and galloped off through the snow.

'Aren't you afraid?' he asked as he loped along.

'For one moment, but never again,' said Molly, and clung on tight to his shaggy white fur.

The Bear took her to a palace as round as a dome. And though it was ice outside, it was warmth and firelight inside, and as cosy as a nest. He gave her robes and ribbons, shoes and books; her plate was always full; and best of all was when the Bear shared their mealtimes and they talked. They talked of earth and sky, of sea and shore. But when the lights burned out and the palace was all dark, Molly reached out to hold his paw, and it was not a paw at all, but a big, gentle hand!

'Bear by day and man by night,' Molly told her sister, 'and as kind as any girl would wish for.' She had only come home to visit her family's new home, where she found them all as rich and round and happy as mudlarks, living in luxury.

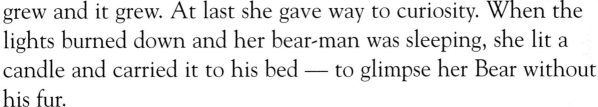

But her sisters, for all their new-found riches, were jealous of Molly's happiness. They dared her, knowing she could never resist a dare: 'Light a light. Look one look. See what it is the darkness hides. You've married a troll, and that's the truth of it!'

She did not want to believe them, but the idea was planted there like a seed in her head, and after she returned from her visit, it grew and it grew and it grew. At last she gave way to curiosity. When the lights burned down and her bear-man was sleeping, she lit a candle and carried it to his bed — to glimpse her Bear without his fur.

'Bless me, if he isn't the handsomest man in all the world!' And her hand shook, so that three drops of candlewax fell on to the young man's shirt.

'What have you done? Oh, Molly, how could you!' he cried in the very moment of opening his eyes. 'If you had cherished me for one whole year, you would have broken her hold over me! But now I must go East of the Sun, West of the Moon. Oh, Molly!' And his eyes reproached her as he melted away — into fur, into snow, into water. The ice palace fell with a crash,

leaving Molly alone in her nightdress on a glacier of ice.

There Molly lifted up her head. 'I'll not rest till I've found you!' she cried, and the frozen sea growled like a bear.

First she wept, but there was no use in weeping.

Then she thought, but there was no good in thinking.

Next she walked, and walking brought her to the house of the East Wind.

'East Wind! O, gentle East Wind! Tell me if you will and if you know: where is the place called East of the Sun, West of the Moon, and how may I get there?'

'I have heard of it,' sighed the mild East Wind, 'but never been there. My brother the West Wind may know; he is stronger.'

So Molly climbed onto the East Wind's back and he carried her far and wide. 'Aren't you afraid, little one?' he asked.

'Only for my Prince,' she said. And when she got down, she found in her hand a golden apple, without knowing how it got there.

At the house of the West Wind she asked again: 'West Wind, O, Wise West Wind! Tell me if you will and if you know: where is the place called East of the Sun, West of the Moon, and how may I get there?'

'I have tasted the scent of it,' said the West Wind, 'but never been there. My brother the South Wind may know; he is stronger and roams farther afield than I.'

So Molly clambered onto the West Wind's back, and he carried her farther and higher. 'Aren't you afraid, little one?' he asked.

'Only for my Prince,' she said. And when she got down, she found in her hand a golden comb without knowing how it got there.

By the time he reached the castle East of the Sun, West of the Moon, the North Wind was winded and hoarse, and could only fling himself face-down and rest till he got back his breath. Molly sat herself down at the foot of the castle wall and played with her golden apple. And when the sun came up, that is what the owner of the castle saw. The owner? A Troll Princess with a nose so long that she tied it in a round-turn-and-two-half-hitches to keep it out of her dinner.

'What's that you have there, beggar maid, and what will you take for it?' called down the Troll Princess, wanting the apple.

'No gold or silver, but a word alone with the Prince who sleeps here,' said Molly, bold as brass.

'I won't deny you that,' said the Troll, but she laughed a nasty laugh, as if she were giving away nothing by it.

Molly was shown to the room where the Prince was staying. Oh, but he was fast asleep! And though she was left alone to shake him and speak in his ear, she could not make him wake.

Next morning, Molly went out and sat by the castle wall, and she combed her hair with the golden comb.

'What's that you have there, beggar maid, and what will you take for it?' called the Troll Princess, wanting the comb.

'Nothing but a word alone with the Prince I saw yesterday,' said Molly.

'I won't deny you that!' said the Troll, but she showed her tombstone teeth in the same nasty grin.

Molly was shown up to the same room, and once again she found her Prince sound asleep. Though she was left alone with him to slap him and shout in his ear —'WAKE UP!' — she could not make him wake. So instead, she pushed a note into his hand, which read, 'Wine drugged: don't drink!'

Next morning Molly was playing again outside the wall, spinning wisps of wool on her golden spindle.

'What's that you have there, beggar maid, and what will you take for it?' called the Troll Princess, wanting the spindle.

'Same as before,' said Molly, and the Troll let her in, knowing she had drugged the Prince's wine and thinking he would not stir.

But this time he was only pretending to be asleep.

'I can't believe you came so far and did so much to find me here!' he whispered, kissing her. 'And all for nothing! Tomorrow I must marry the Troll Princess with her nose in a knot, and nothing can save me!'

'Love can save anyone,' said Molly, 'and here's how . . .'

Next day, Molly sat outside the wall, as ragged as ever. But indoors, the Troll Princess came down to her wedding in silken finery, her nose tied in a bow and her hair fastened back with a silver cartwheel. Ever so many troll maidens tripped behind her in boots as big as boats. But the bridegroom arrived only half-dressed.

'I can't marry you in this shirt!' he complained. 'Someone has dropped three spots of candlewax on it — see here! Wash it for me, won't you, as you'll wash it when we are married.'

Though washing was not to her liking, the Troll Princess flung her nose over her shoulder and dunked the shirt up and down in a tub of soapy water. But the more she washed it the blacker it grew, till a crow could have worn it to a funeral.

'D'you call that washing?' demanded the Prince. 'There's a beggar maid at the door could do better than that!' And he called in Molly.

So Molly washed the shirt, washed it in the sea, and it became so white a dove could have worn it to a wedding.

'Ah now, this is the girl I shall marry!' said the Prince.

When they held hands, the malice of the trolls ran off them like water off a swan, and the trolls grew so mad with rage that one by one they went off – BANG! – so that ordinary people like you and I thought they saw shooting stars East of the Sun, West of the Moon, and made a wish.

Molly and her Prince sailed away in the shoe of the Troll Princess, towing the other behind, full of treasure. And the four winds sped them on their way, calling out to the Prince, 'Aren't you afraid of such a daring wife?'

The Prince replied, 'Only of parting from her, and that I will never do!'

PRINCESS DORA AND THE MINISTERS OF STATE

When the King of Ufonia decided to go to the World Congress, he said to his daughter, 'No need to worry, Dora. My ministers of state will look after everything while I'm gone.'

But his ministers threw up their hands in protest.

'I should go to the World Congress — a man of my stature!' said the fat Prime Minister.

'I should be there to advise His Majesty — a man of my worth!' said the Chancellor, gripping the lapels of the expensive fur coat he always wore.

'I should, you mean,' said the Home Secretary, uncrossing her long, elegant legs. The King looked troubled.

'Don't worry, Father,' said Princess Dora. 'I shall be quite all right on my own. You all go. After all, what can happen while you're gone?'

And so they all drove away, the coach swaying under the weight of so many great people.

While the Princess was still waving her handkerchief, she felt a drop of rain fall on her nose, and ran to fetch in the royal washing.

After the rain came hail and sleet and snow. Never in the history of Ufonia had the people seen such weather. Hurricanes blew off their chimneys, and the rivers swelled to bursting.

'What must I do?' said Princess Dora to her dog. 'If only I had some ministers of state to advise me.' The royal bloodhound yawned. 'You're right, Bludnock, I must appoint new ministers to save the city. Let me see. First a Chancellor.'

'And how do we choose a Chancellor?' asked the bloodhound.

'Well, the last one,' said Dora, 'had the biggest fur coat I ever saw. Find the biggest fur coat, and the person inside it is bound to be a good Chancellor.'

'And the Home Secretary?'

'Well, the last one,' said Dora, 'had the longest legs I've ever seen. Find someone with long legs and she is bound to make a good Home Secretary.'

'Prime Minister?' said the bloodhound, taking notes.

'Well, the last one,' said Dora, 'was the fattest man in the kingdom. If we look for someone huge, we can't go wrong!'

So the Princess and the bloodhound put on their waterproofs and waded out into the teeth of the gale. They searched high and low, and near and far, but the biggest fur coat they could find belonged to a polar bear.

Meanwhile, the trees were tumbling, barns collapsing, and ships were driven ashore with sheets of ice where their sails should have been. The people sobbed with cold, and wailed, 'Where's the Princess? How will she save us?'

Princess Dora and the bloodhound were, in fact, searching hither and thither, up hill and down dale, for a Home Secretary. But the longest legs they could find belonged to a giraffe.

Meanwhile, the reservoir in the mountains above Ufonia City was more full of rain and snow and sleet than it had ever been. The dam which held back the water groaned and bellied outwards like a great bow window. If it burst,

the whole country would be flooded as high as the highest church spire. The people jibbered with cold and fright: 'Where is the Princess? How could she desert us at a time like this? We'll all be drowned!'

Dora had not deserted them, nor had the royal bloodhound.

They were busy searching willi-cum-nether and over-li-do for a Prime Minister. Unfortunately, the fattest they could find was a hippopotamus blowing bubbles in the mud.

Dora hurried home to Ufonia City. As they went, she explained the danger her country faced to her new ministers of state.

'Of course, we have no experience of government,' said the polar bear, 'but we will do what we can.'

Just as they approached the city, there was a crack like the end of the world, and a zigzag line appeared from top to bottom of the dam. Everyone who could, climbed onto their roof.

The hippopotamus trotted as fast as he was able, and sat down with his flank against the dam. The pent-up water pushed against him, but could not get past.

Then the giraffe waded through the town, with Dora on her back, her legs so long that the floodwater rushed under her ribs. She rescued small boys from lamp posts, farmers from trees, babies from cradles washed away on the flood.

She carried them all to the palace (which stood on a hill) and went back for more. Soon everyone in Ufonia City lay in a damp heap on the ballroom floor, while the blizzard blew snow in at the windows and the wind howled up and down the spiral stairs.

The polar bear Chancellor spread his paws and clasped them close. He was as warm as an electric blanket, and silky soft. His breath filled the palace with a comforting smell of fish, and his big paws stroked the children till they fell asleep.

The storms blew themselves out that night. When the King and his ministers of state came back from the World Congress, there was hardly a snowdrift or a puddle to show for the great gales. But the whole town rang to the banging of hammers and the clang of scaffolding as people repaired their homes and mended the dam.

'There is a hippopotamus sitting in my office!' complained the Prime Minister furiously.

'Yes,' said Dora. 'I needed a little help while you were gone.'

'There's a giraffe riding in my limousine!' said the Home Secretary, greatly put out.

'Yes,' said Dora. 'She was such a help while you weren't here.'

'There is a polar bear in the counting house!' screamed the Chancellor, running in with his fur coat in tatters.

'Yes,' said Dora. 'He helped me save the city while you were away.'

And when the King heard what had happened during his absence, he said he would not be going to any World Congresses in future, in case his people needed him. 'My ministers of state can go in my place,' he said.

And so they did. In fact, the King entrusted the polar bear, the giraffe and the hippopotamus with all manner of important jobs.

But I have no idea what became of the fat man, the lady with the long legs, or the man who wore his fur coat all year round.

MOUSEY AND SULKY PUSS

'Hear ye! Hear ye! Let it be known in every corner of the land, that a daughter is born to the King and Queen of Bellepays! Let no-one work today, for the King declares this a public holiday!'

At the sound of the herald's announcement, everyone ran out into the streets and began to dance and sing. But when the invitations were sent out for the royal christening of the baby Princess, a terrible mistake was made.

No-one invited Agatha!

Agatha had not always been a crabbed and spiteful witch. But ever since the day she turned her sister by mistake into a large black cat, Agatha had not smiled. Neither had her sister, come to that. In fact her sister was such a sad sack of a cat that she was known as Sulky Puss. Agatha searched the world over for a magic spell which would restore her sister to human form, and it was while she was away on one such trip that Princess Marcia was born. That's why *no-one invited Agatha.*

On the day of the christening, all manner of important and famous people travelled to the celebrations. So did Agatha. She waited until all the other christening presents had been given — spoons and egg cups and china bowls — then she did her worst.

'Because you made little of me, I shall make little of your precious Princess!' cried Agatha, and struck the crib with her wand. When the purple smoke cleared, Agatha had gone, and there in the royal cradle wriggled — a small white mouse.

The Mouse Princess they called her — or Mousey for short. And Mousey was very, very short. Her dresses could be made from a single silk handkerchief, her bed from an open jewel box. She was as pleasant a little thing as you could ever hope to meet — but she was, when all's said, a white mouse who ate cheese with her paws and whiffled her small, pink nose.

The King, terrified for her safety, banished every cat from Bellepays, with one single exception. Sulky Puss, the witch's sister, was allowed to stay because no-one dared tell her to go. Besides, she was a vegetarian.

As the years passed, the other baby girls in Bellepays grew into lovely young women. But Mousey only grew into a lovely young mouse. When she was in a room, it was easy to overlook her, to forget she was there. She squeaked so quietly that she was rarely heard. And not everyone was as kind and as loving as the King and Queen. Some were ashamed to admit they had a mouse for a Princess, and did their best to forget all about her. Just as Agatha had not been invited to the christening, *no-one invited Mousey anywhere.*

Then, as in all such stories and histories, the Prince of the next door kingdom announced his wish to choose a bride.

'Oyez! Oyez! Every maiden of wealth or degree is invited to the palace of the King of Oystria, so that the Prince Michelangelo may have dancing partners at the Grand Ball!'

What queues there were at the dress shops, at the milliners, the hairdressers and the florists! There were carriages at every door and women arrayed in every colour of the rainbow scrambling to be ready in time for the Grand Ball.

'I should like to go, too,' said Mousey, but nobody heard her. She climbed onto the dinner table and shouted as loud as she was able, 'I want to go, too!'

'Nonsense, Mousey dear,' said the Queen. 'You would get trodden on.'

'Besides, there are still cats in Oystria,' said the King. 'Out of the question. Get down off the table, please.'

But the more they said no, the more determined Mousey became to go to the Ball. She put on her finest silk handkerchief dress — it was scarlet with silver embroidery — and a sash made from a velvet hair ribbon. She fetched a pin — to use as a sword if she met any cats — and put on her tiny tiara, then ran to the palace door.

But she was only in time to see the coach, with her mother and father in it, gathering speed as it drove away from the palace down the long, dusty drive.

Mousey sat down and wept.

Then she got up and dried her tears. How could she make the journey to Oystria? By boat?

She found her father's newspaper and folded it ever so many times, until she had made a paper boat. She dragged it to the moat and rowed it out to where the moat joined the winding river which flowed right across both countries. But she had forgotten — the river flowed OUT of Oystria and INTO Bellepays. It was running in the wrong direction!

Mousey paddled ashore and thought again. She would fly to Oystria! But though she was able to fold a paper glider out of the newspaper, she could not get it up the winding stairs to the castle parapet.

She went to the stable, where the royal horses were kept. But the huge mares and stallions towered over her like monsters, and she dared not stay among those swinging hooves for fear she may be trampled and never seen again.

'What I need is a horse more suited to my size,' thought Mousey, and as she crept out of the stable door, she saw the very thing.

A dozen chickens were pecking in the yard, and there beside the dungheap, a splendid red cockerel stretched its claws and surveyed its farmyard kingdom.

Mousey took the sash from her dress, ran full tilt up the dungheap, and launched herself onto the back of the cockerel. The bird was so startled that it set off to run. And after Mousey had got the ribbon into its beak for reins, it was just a matter of guiding the speeding fowl in the direction of the Oystrian border.

The Grand Ball was well underway when Mousey arrived, riding her cockerel. She did not dismount at the gate, nor at the steps, but rode straight on up, for fear the footmen and flunkies thought she was an ordinary house mouse. Indoors, she came to a scarlet-carpeted staircase lit by chandeliers. At the foot of the stairs, she could just make out the Prince.

She missed seeing Sulky Puss.

Oh yes, Sulky Puss was there. The King of Oystria had not made the same mistake as his neighbour. He had remembered to invite Agatha, and Agatha had brought her cat.

Sulky Puss saw the cockerel with its reins of scarlet velvet. She saw the meal-sized white mouse on its back, damp at the hems, stained black with newsprint, tiara awry over her little pink eyes, pin-sized sword raised aloft and tiny mouth open to shout: 'Out of the way! Out of the way! I don't know how to stop this bird!'

It was enough to make a cat laugh.

And that's just what Sulky Puss did. For the first time in her miserable sad-sack cat's nine lives, Sulky Puss rolled on her back in fits of giggles.

The music in the ballroom faltered and fell silent.

Everyone stared. For there, rolling on her back on the staircase, in a most unladylike way, was a large fat witch, laughing and laughing and laughing.

'Sister!' cried Agatha joyously. 'The spell! It's lifted!'

'All I needed was a good laugh,' said Anastasia wiping her eyes and scratching some cat food off her dress. 'And that sight was enough to give me one!'

Agatha looked to see what jester or clown had restored her sister to her. And when she recognized the Mouse Princess, she was filled with tender remorse for the unkindness she had done at the christening.

And she hit Mousey with her wand.

The white mouse flew through the air, somersaulting one, two, three times before landing at the feet of the Prince of Oystria. She landed heavily, perhaps because she was no longer a mouse but a tall, elegant, pale-skinned girl in a ball dress of red silk, with ash-blonde hair tumbling down from a buckled tiara.

'Good gracious,' said the Prince. 'You are the most beautiful young lady I have seen all night. Will you marry me?'

'No, thank you,' said Marcia. 'I just wanted to dance.'

So that's what they did instead.